P9-ELT-943

E
E

Emberley, Barbara

Drummer Hoff

$12.95

DATE			
SEP 28			
MAR 1 0			
NOV 2 1 1994			
APR 13			
DEC 1 2			
OCT 0 1 1997			

Z-6642

© THE BAKER & TAYLOR CO.

DRUMMER HOFF

LAKESHORE SCHOOL LIBRARY

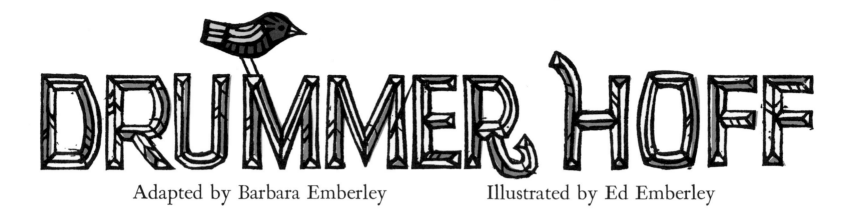

DRUMMER HOFF

Adapted by Barbara Emberley   Illustrated by Ed Emberley

Simon and Schuster Books for Young Readers
Published by Simon & Schuster Inc., New York

Z-6642   6/91

Copyright © 1967 by Edward R. Emberley and Barbara Emberley.
All rights reserved including the right of reproduction in whole or in part in any form.
Published by Simon and Schuster Books for Young Readers, A Division of Simon & Schuster, Inc.
Simon & Schuster Building, Rockefeller Center, 1230 Avenue of the Americas, New York, NY 10020

20   19   18   17

30   29   28   27   26   25   24   23   pbk

Simon and Schuster Books for Young Readers is a trademark of Simon & Schuster, Inc.
Manufactured in the United States of America

Library of Congress Cataloging-in-Publication Data

Emberley, Barbara.
Drummer Hoff.
Summary: A cumulative folk song in which seven
soldiers build a magnificent cannon, but Drummer
Hoff fires it off.
[1. Folk songs]   I. Emberley, Ed. ill. II. Title.
PZ8.3.E515Dr 1987   784.4′05   87-35755
ISBN 0-671-66248-1   ISBN 0-671-66249-X (pbk.)

Drummer Hoff fired it off.

Private Parriage
brought the carriage,

but Drummer Hoff fired it off.

Corporal Farrell
brought the barrel.

Corporal Farrell
brought the barrel,
Private Parriage
brought the carriage,
but Drummer Hoff
fired it off.

Sergeant Chowder
brought the powder.

Sergeant Chowder
brought the powder,
Corporal Farrell
brought the barrel,
Private Parriage
brought the carriage,
but Drummer Hoff
fired it off.

Captain Bammer
brought the rammer.

Captain Bammer
brought the rammer,
Sergeant Chowder
brought the powder,
Corporal Farrell
brought the barrel,
Private Parriage
brought the carriage,
but Drummer Hoff fired it off.

Major Scott
brought the shot.

Major Scott brought the shot,
Captain Bammer
brought the rammer,
Sergeant Chowder
brought the powder,
Corporal Farrell
brought the barrel,
Private Parriage
brought the carriage,
but Drummer Hoff fired it off.

General Border
gave the order.

General Border
gave the order,
Major Scott
brought the shot,
Captain Bammer
brought the rammer,
Sergeant Chowder
brought the powder,
Corporal Farrell
brought the barrel,
Private Parriage
brought the carriage,
but Drummer Hoff fired it off.